W9-AXN-748

# JOSHUA and the BIG BAD BLUE CRABS

by Mark Childress

Illustrated by Mary Barrett Brown

**Little, Brown and Company**
Boston   New York   Toronto   London

Also by Mark Childress
*Joshua and Bigtooth*

Also illustrated by Mary Barrett Brown
*Great Northern Diver: The Loon*
*Playful Slider: The North American River Otter*

For Joshua, Ani, and Steven.
Also for Emma, Sarah, Mary Va., Bonnie D., Joey,
Isaac, J.C., Bailey, Anna C., Hannah,
and all future Malleteers.
M. C.

To Barbaranne and Ralph, who keep filling the trunk with treasures.
And to my two Joshuas: Sam and Geoff, as well as Bevy, Porter, Kelly,
Dottie, George Jr., Tyler, and Don (the river captain) — thank you.
M. B. B.

First Edition

Childress, Mark.
   Joshua and the big bad blue crabs / by Mark Childress ;
illustrated by Mary Barrett Brown. — 1st ed.
      p.      cm.
   Summary: Joshua sets off to deliver a huckleberry pie to his grandmother
and he and the pie are kidnapped by a mob of mean-tempered crabs.
   ISBN 0-316-14118-6
   [1. Crabs — Fiction.] I. Brown, Mary Barrett, ill. II. Title.
PZ7.C44124Jp   1996
[Fic] — dc20                                                 93-30351

10  9  8  7  6  5  4  3  2  1

NIL

Published simultaneously in Canada
by Little, Brown & Company (Canada) Limited

Printed in Italy

It was a summer day, steamy and lazy and hot. Joshua paddled his boat up the Magnolia River. He was going to Granny's to deliver a huckleberry pie Mama had made. The pie smelled wonderful. Mama made the very best huckleberry pies in the world.

The magnolia trees wore their dressiest white blossoms. This was a magical river, full of fish and friendly alligators and things that went *splash!* Every summer morning, Joshua pulled two or three fat blue crabs from the trap at the dock. Every afternoon, birds played tag in the air.

Joshua paddled around the bend where a giant live oak tree touched its elbows to the water. He could taste that huckleberry pie already. He hoped Granny had ice cream to go with it.

Joshua jumped out to tie up his boat, but the rope slithered through his hands. "Hey, wait!" he cried. But the boat didn't hear him. It floated under its own power all the way to the middle of the river — pie and all.

Joshua shucked off his shirt. He pinched his nose and leapt into the chilly green water. He was a strong swimmer, but the boat stayed just out of his reach. He stopped to catch his breath. The boat stopped. When he started swimming again, the boat started moving again. Then he saw what was making it move....

The water was alive with crabs — a whole army of mean-looking crabs! They were big. They were blue. They were bad. Their wicked pinchers were locked on the hull. They were kidnapping Joshua's boat!

The boat bumped the shore. The big bad blue crabs swarmed
all over it, snapping their pinchers. They looked hungry,
not friendly. A squadron of crabs hustled in and lifted the
huckleberry pie onto their shoulders. Other crabs locked
pinchers together to form a bridge. The pie scuttled across
the bridge to the shore. The boat began to drift away.

Joshua dashed after his boat. The pie marched away up the riverbank at the head of a parade of overjoyed crabs. They strutted and celebrated and clicked their pinchers.

By the time Joshua got to the shore, the crabs were gone. The pie plate sat on a tree stump, shiny and clean as the day Mama brought it home from the store. Joshua was too ashamed to go to Granny's. He floated home on the current. He was mad at those crabs. What had he ever done to them? They had no right to kidnap that pie, even if it was the very best huckleberry pie in the world.

At first Mama didn't believe him. "I've never known crabs to have a taste for huckleberries," she said. "Sure you didn't get hungry and eat it yourself?" Joshua swore he hadn't. "Well, I'll make another pie for Granny," Mama said, "if you clean out the boathouse, paint the shed, mend the cast nets, sweep the porch, pull the weeds, and bring in some firewood."

That seemed like an awful lot of work to Joshua, but it had
been a very fine pie, after all. Mama rolled out another piecrust
while Joshua cleaned and scrubbed and painted and mended
and sweated. He stayed mad at those crabs. They had him
outnumbered — a whole big bad crab army against one boy.
He plotted revenge.

The next morning, Joshua built a wooden pie box with a latch and a padlock. He put the box in his boat. In his knapsack he carried a new straw hat for Granny and a special surprise for the crabs. He set out upriver. A flock of geese flew by in a perfect V. At the live oak tree, the water began to stir. Joshua peered over the side. A flotilla of crabs nipped the air with their pinchers. Their eyes bugged out on stalks from their heads. They seemed to gaze hungrily toward the wooden box.

Joshua hopped onto Granny's dock. The crabs swarmed into
the boat, surrounding the pie box. One crab picked the
lock with the tip of its claw. More crabs lifted the lid, licking
their chops.
Surprise! The box was empty, except for a note from Joshua.
Joshua patted the knapsack on his shoulder and laughed.
They had him outnumbered — but he had them outsmarted.
At least, that's what he thought....

The pie was in his knapsack, all right, but in the excitement it had flipped over, smearing huckleberries all over Granny's new straw hat. She took a taste on her finger. "Mighty good pie," she said. "I wouldn't mess around with crabs if I were you."

The next day was Joshua's birthday. He had so much fun
at his party, he forgot all about his war with the crabs.
All the kids from the river came to the log cabin to play
pin-the-tail-on-the-donkey and bob for apples. Joshua got
a wonderful present from Mama and Daddy: an actual
store-bought rod and reel!

That evening Granny rowed over for a special birthday supper.
Mama made a big pot of crab gumbo, Joshua's favorite. Tonight,
though, he felt a little funny about eating it. He just tasted the
broth, then sat back to wait for dessert.

"Joshua, I baked you a birthday cake," Granny said, "but it
disappeared from my windowsill this morning. It was
chocolate, with coconut frosting."

Mama looked at Joshua curiously. "You know, a lot of sweet
things have been turning up missing," she said. "I think
somebody around here has a sweet tooth."

Joshua went out to dump the empty crab shells in the river.
Now he was really mad. He'd gotten the blame for two pies *and*
a birthday cake, which he never even got to taste. Bending over
the water, he noticed three big blue crabs watching him.
Tears ran down their eyestalks. The sight of those crab shells
splashing into the river was making them cry. One of them
waved a tiny white flag.
Poor crabs. Suddenly Joshua felt sorry for fighting with them
and for liking crab gumbo so much. No wonder crabs turned
out so mad and so bad, with the crab trap and the boiling pot
waiting for them! So they wanted a little dessert! Was that
too much to ask — if you were the main course?

"Boys, I'll make you a deal," Joshua said. "I'll stop eating crab gumbo if you promise you won't steal any more pies or cakes. Okay?" The crabs clicked their pinchers in agreement. Joshua went to bed happy that night. The war seemed to be over. He dreamed peaceful summertime dreams of the river.

The next day, Joshua paddled out to practice casting his new
fishing rod. It took a few tries to learn the right way to hold his
thumb, but before long his hook was sailing halfway across
the river and landing *plop!* just where he wanted it.
Suddenly the boat began to move. Joshua knelt in the bow.
Surrounded! The crab army, two hundred strong! "Hey, I'm all
out of pies," he pleaded. "Can't you please leave me alone?"
But the crabs pushed the boat all the way to the riverbank.
They didn't look mad today, or especially bad. They marched
out of the water and up the bank in a cheerful procession,
three by three.

Joshua followed them. Stepping over a fallen log, he came into a clearing. A thousand crabs were having a party. A crab combo clicked out a hot calypso rhythm. Crab dancers twirled and shimmied on the dance floor. A few wallflower crabs hung around at the back, acting shy.

A lovely crab couple whirled past. The band played "The Gumbo Limbo." A circle of crabs scuttled in bearing a beautiful cake with white frosting, and a special message spelled out in huckleberries. A big daddy crab sliced the cake with his sharp pincher. Joshua got the first piece. Chocolate, with coconut frosting. Very tasty. Maybe the best birthday cake in the world.

The crabs had been mad once, and they had been bad once,
but they sure knew how to throw a party. Joshua made a whole
army of new friends.

Joshua didn't see much of the crabs after that. He learned to like other kinds of gumbo. If he had any pies to deliver, he carried them across the bridge to Granny's, the long way around. And if on a summer morning he found a stray crab in his trap, Joshua always let it get away.